Usborne
Great Britain
Quiz Book

Sam Smith

Illustrated by El primo Ramón

Designed by Kate Rimmer

1

1 **What is the Welsh name for Wales?**
   a) Alba   b) Cymru   c) Éire

2 **I was a famous English scientist and mathematician. My theory of gravity was supposedly inspired by an apple falling on my head.** Who am I? *Isaac Newton*

3 **Public phone boxes in Britain are traditionally...**
   a) red   b) blue   c) green

4 **What is the name of the bridge below? Its road can be raised to allow ships to pass underneath.**
   a) London Bridge
   b) Putney Bridge
   c) Tower Bridge

5 What did King John sign at Runnymede in 1215: the Magna Carta **or** the Domesday Book?

6 Where in England can you visit the house where William Shakespeare was born?

  a) Stratford-upon-Avon

  b) Winchester

  c) Oxford

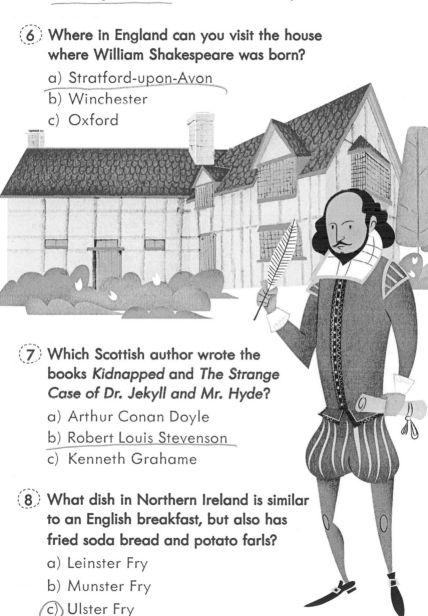

7 Which Scottish author wrote the books *Kidnapped* and *The Strange Case of Dr. Jekyll and Mr. Hyde*?

  a) Arthur Conan Doyle

  b) Robert Louis Stevenson

  c) Kenneth Grahame

8 What dish in Northern Ireland is similar to an English breakfast, but also has fried soda bread and potato farls?

  a) Leinster Fry

  b) Munster Fry

  c) Ulster Fry

1. **If you ordered "bangers and mash" from a British menu, what would be served with your mashed potato?**

   a) meatballs   b) pork chops   c) sausages

2. **I was built to celebrate the new millennium. I turn slowly on the South Bank, and offer my passengers spectacular views of the London skyline.** What am I?

   London Eye

3. **There is a £1 million banknote.** True or false?

4. **Who was the fictional Englishman whose travels took him to the land of Lilliput, ruled by tiny people, and the land of Brobdingnag, ruled by giant people?**

   a) Phileas Fogg   b) Robinson Crusoe   c) Gulliver

5. **When is St. David's Day celebrated in Wales?**

   a) March 1st   b) March 17th   c) April 23rd

6. **Which river is the longest in Great Britain?**

   a) Mersey
   b) Severn
   c) Trent

7. Which pair of sporting rivals are known as the Old Firm: Celtic and Rangers **or** Everton and Liverpool?

8. The women who campaigned for women's voting rights in Britain in the early 1900s were known as...

a) Feminists   b) Pankhursts   c) Suffragettes

9. What is the name of Great Britain's only venomous snake?

a) adder   b) cobra   c) mamba

10. Which lake or loch is said to be home to a prehistoric monster?

a) Lake Windermere
b) Loch Lomond
c) Loch Ness

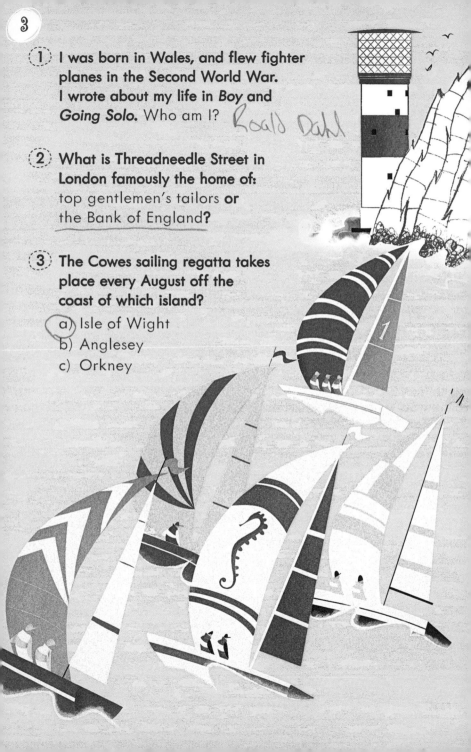

3

1. I was born in Wales, and flew fighter planes in the Second World War. I wrote about my life in *Boy* and *Going Solo*. Who am I? *Roald Dahl*

2. What is Threadneedle Street in London famously the home of: top gentlemen's tailors **or** the Bank of England?

3. The Cowes sailing regatta takes place every August off the coast of which island?
   a) Isle of Wight
   b) Anglesey
   c) Orkney

(4) ... And what is the name of the line of jagged chalk rocks that some boats in the regatta race around?

　　a) the Claws　　　b) the Teeth　　　c) the Needles

(5) In 2013, which Welsh winger became the most expensive player in history when Real Madrid signed him for a world record fee of £85.1 million?

　　a) Aaron Ramsey　　b) Gareth Bale　　c) Ryan Giggs

(6) With which famous flag is the Englishman Calico Jack associated: the Jolly Roger **or** the Union Jack?

(7) "Glen" is the Scottish word for what?

　　a) a hill　　　b) a valley　　　c) a forest

1 What is the capital city of Scotland?

a) Glasgow   b) Aberdeen   c) Edinburgh

2 Which island hosts a famous motorcycle race called the Tourist Trophy (TT) each year?

a) Isle of Man   b) Isle of Wight   c) Isle of Skye

3 On a standard British Monopoly board, which property is the most expensive?

a) Leicester Square   b) Mayfair   c) Pall Mall

4 Which word can follow Dundee, Eccles and Welsh to make the names of three baked British foods?

a) bread   b) cake   c) pie

5 What's the name of the living attraction in Cornwall with giant domes full of plants from around the world?

a) Paradise Project   b) Eden Project   c) Utopia Project

6 What is the huge sculpture below called, which you can see as you head north past Gateshead?

    a) The Steel Sentinel
    b) The Gateshead Giant
    c) The Angel of the North

7 For how long was Lady Jane Grey the Queen of England: nine days **or** nine years?

8 Who is the world-famous playwright whose works include *Romeo and Juliet* and *Hamlet*? Shakespear

9 How many British astronauts have walked on the Moon?

    a) ten   b) two   c) none

10 Which of these is the name of a real village in England: Great Snoring **or** Little Sleeping?

1 Great Britain is nicknamed The Emerald Isle.
True or false?

2 What do the Welsh use to make laverbread?

a) maggots   b) seaweed   c) volcanic rock

3 *Rocket*, built by English engineer George Stephenson, was an early form of what?

a) car   b) train   c) spacecraft

4 In 1996, scientists in Scotland created the world's first cloned mammal – a sheep. What was her name?

a) Dolly   b) Molly   c) Polly

5 In which battle was the Anglo-Saxon king Harold Godwinson killed by an arrow through the eye?

a) Stamford Bridge
b) Bannockburn
c) Hastings

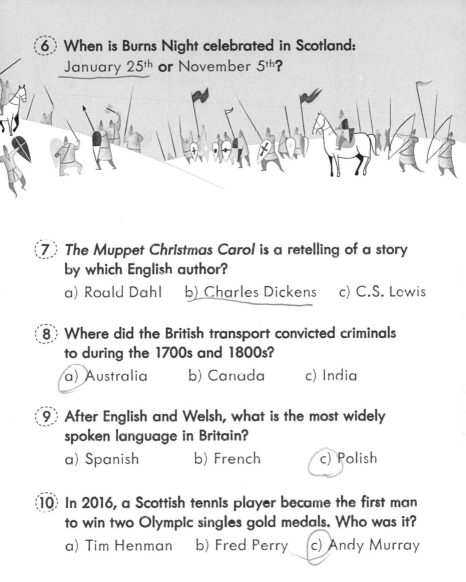

6. When is Burns Night celebrated in Scotland: January 25th <u>or</u> November 5th?

7. *The Muppet Christmas Carol* is a retelling of a story by which English author?

   a) Roald Dahl   b) <u>Charles Dickens</u>   c) C.S. Lewis

8. Where did the British transport convicted criminals to during the 1700s and 1800s?

   a) Australia   b) Canada   c) India

9. After English and Welsh, what is the most widely spoken language in Britain?

   a) Spanish   b) French   c) Polish

10. In 2016, a Scottish tennis player became the first man to win two Olympic singles gold medals. Who was it?

    a) Tim Henman   b) Fred Perry   c) Andy Murray

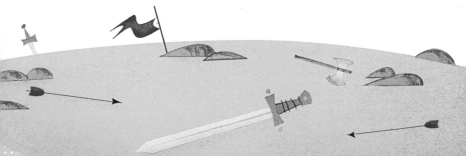

1 What spectacular stunt did the Queen appear to do in the opening ceremony for the London 2012 Olympics?

a) skydive into the stadium
b) waterski along the Thames
c) walk a tightrope over the crowd

2 What skirt-like clothes do Scotsmen traditionally wear?

a) kilts   b) kelpies   c) kegs

3 The Ashes cricket series has been contested for over 100 years between England and which other country?

a) India   b) Australia   c) South Africa

4 Who married Prince Charles and became known as the People's Princess... but was tragically killed in a car crash?

5 "Victoria Cross" is the name of what?

a) a dog breed Queen Victoria liked
b) a London Underground station
c) a military service medal

6 Which show shares its name with a naval flag, and is the world's longest-running children's TV show?

B _ _ _   P _ _ _ _

7 In an Old English poem, which monster does Beowulf kill?

a) Grendel   b) Medusa   c) Shelob

8 Why was King Ethelred known as "the Unready"?

a) he was killed in a surprise attack
b) he came to the throne very young
c) he was badly advised during his reign

9 The steam locomotive below is taking tourists up the highest mountain in Wales. What's the mountain's name?

a) Helvellyn   b) Snowdon   c) Scafell Pike

1. Ships in the British Royal Navy often have HMS at the start of their names. What does HMS stand for?

a) Homeland Maritime Service
b) High Mistress of the Seas
c) Her Majesty's Ship

2. In *Watership Down,* Hazel's younger brother shares his name with which slang term for an amount of British money?

a) Quid
b) Fiver
c) Tenner

3. Which London building is protected by guards like the one on the right?

a) Tower of London
b) Buckingham Palace
c) Houses of Parliament

4. Sticking a postage stamp on upside down is an act of treason in Britain.

True or false?

5. Manx cats are a type of cat from the Isle of Man. What don't they have?

a) claws
b) tails
c) fur

6 In 1866, the ships *Ariel* and *Taeping* left China and raced over 14,000 miles to be first back to London. After more than three months at sea, how far apart did they finish?

a) 28 minutes   b) 28 hours   c) 28 days

7 Which word follows Hamilton to make the name of a sports team from Scotland?

a) Intellectual   b) Educational   c) Academical

8 Which English record producer is famous for his roles as a judge on *Britain's Got Talent* and *The X Factor*?

a) Michael McIntyre
b) Simon Cowell
c) Piers Morgan

9 What are the black, furry hats worn by the Queen's Guard called?

a) bearskins
b) deerstalkers
c) squirreltails

10 What is the Welsh slang name for a microwave?

a) bobbity bing
b) dopsy ding
c) popty ping

1 In which city's shipyards was
the *Titanic* built and fitted out?

a) Dundee
b) Portsmouth
c) Belfast

2 Which of these is NOT a nickname of a London skyscraper?

a) knitting needle   b) cheese grater   c) walkie-talkie

3 Skomer Island, off the coast of Wales, is home to a
huge colony of which water birds?

a) pelicans   b) penguins   c) puffins

4 In *His Dark Materials*, by Philip Pullman, what is the name
of the fictional Oxford college where Lyra grows up?

a) Jordan   b) Oriel   c) Somerville

5 I am famous for my beautiful lakes and for having the
highest mountain in England. I inspired the settings
for many of Beatrix Potter's stories.

Which region am I?

6 What are Samson and Goliath in Northern Ireland?

    a) mountains   b) cranes   c) statues

7 A dog named Pickles became famous in 1966 when he found what hidden in a hedge?

    a) the Crown Jewels

    b) the World Cup

    c) the *Mona Lisa*

8 Which of these traditional Scottish dishes is NOT a kind of soup?

    a) cullen skink

    b) cock-a-leekie

    c) cranachan

1. **What is the name of the traditional Scottish dish that is made from various types of sheep's meat?**

   a) shepherd's pie   b) lasagne   c) haggis

2. **My friend is Doctor Watson, and my enemy is the Napoleon of crime. I live at 221B Baker Street.** Who am I?

3. **In 2014, which golfer from Northern Ireland became only the third player ever to win three majors by the age of 25:** Graeme McDowell **or** Rory McIlroy?

4. **On reaching 100 years old, a British citizen can...**

   a) have a street in their town named after them
   b) receive a personal message from the Queen
   c) become an honorary lord/lady of the realm

5) The Channel Tunnel links England to which country?

    a) France   b) Germany   c) Spain

6) Which area of London hosts a world-famous flower show each year?

    a) Bloomsbury   b) Primrose Hill   c) Chelsea

7) Which Scottish actor played the Jedi Knight Obi-Wan Kenobi in the three *Star Wars* prequels?

    a) Ewan McGregor   b) Peter Capaldi   c) James McAvoy

8) Which Roman emperor built a huge wall across northern Britain in 122 AD?

    a) Nero   b) Hadrian   c) Vespasian

1 Who did Prince William marry in 2012?

a) Catherine Upperton
b) Catherine Middleton
c) Catherine Lowerton

2 Which sea around Britain is known for its many oil platforms?

a) North Sea
b) Irish Sea
c) Celtic Sea

3 Which of these drinks was originally invented in England?

a) Coca-Cola
b) Champagne
c) Coffee

4 If you cycled from the northeast tip of mainland Britain at John o' Groats to the southwest tip at Land's End, roughly how far would you have gone?

a) 85 miles   b) 850 miles   c) 8,500 miles

5 Who is a famous British graffiti artist: Banksy **or** Pudsey?

6 What is the name of the international rugby team that represents all of Great Britain and Ireland?

a) Wasps   b) Dragons   c) Lions

7 Where in the West Country has a world-famous music festival been held annually since 1981?

a) Bournemouth
b) Glastonbury
c) St. Ives

8 "The castle capital of the world" is a nickname of which country?

a) England   b) Scotland
c) Wales   d) Northern Ireland

9 Which animal completes these famous lines by the English poet William Blake?

"_____, _____ burning bright,
In the forests of the night."

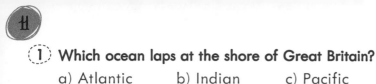

1 Which ocean laps at the shore of Great Britain?

a) Atlantic   b) Indian   c) Pacific

2 I live in the English countryside with my wife and four children. Three farmers called Boggis, Bunce and Bean try to catch me, but I'm too clever for them. Who am I?

3 "Bring me my Chariot of fire" is a line from a patriotic English song that shares its name with which ancient city?

a) Constantinople   b) Jerusalem   c) Alexandria

4 Where in Scotland is the "Home of Golf"?

a) Gleneagles   b) Muirfield   c) St. Andrews

5 The men below are recreating a contest in which knights used to charge at each other with wooden lances. Was this sport called: sparring **or** jousting?

6 Which side of the road do people drive on in Wales?

7 "Capability" Brown, as he was known, is famous for designing many of England's finest parks and gardens. What was his real name?

a) Bedivere   b) Galahad   c) Lancelot

8 Which king built Warwick Castle in 1068?

a) William I
b) Richard II
c) Edward III

Pair up the words below to make the names of six British foods. Then do the same on the opposite page to make the names of six more.

1) Cumberland

2) Stargazy

4) Lancashire

3) Shropshire

5) Cornish

6) Beef

a) Blue

b) Pasty

c) Hotpot

f) Pie

d) Sausage

e) Wellington

1) Eton

2) Banoffee

3) Victoria

4) Bakewell

5) Jam

6) Knickerbocker

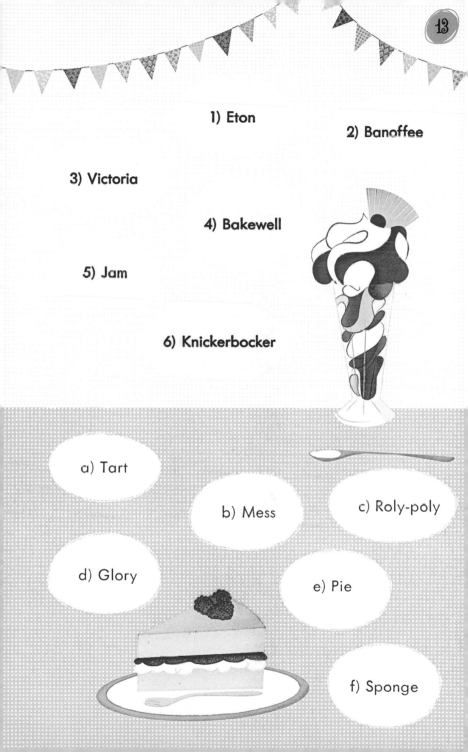

a) Tart

b) Mess

c) Roly-poly

d) Glory

e) Pie

f) Sponge

1 Which breed of cattle is NOT from Scotland?

    a) Aberdeen Angus   b) Hereford   c) Highland

2 Match each invention to its British creator:

    a) television   1) Tim Berners-Lee

    b) telephone   2) John Logie Baird

    c) world wide web   3) Alexander Graham Bell

3 In 1588, Sir Francis Drake helped defend England against the Spanish Armada. But what did he supposedly complete a game of before he set sail: bowls **or** battleships?

4 Where in London could you see the parade shown below?

    a) Chinatown   b) Japantown   c) Thaitown

5 Nearly all bananas sold in supermarkets are perfect clones of bananas that were grown in **Derbyshire.** True or false?

6 Which boy who never grows up did Scottish author J.M. Barrie write about?

P _ _ _ _   P _ _

7 In Victorian times, cheap, dramatic stories were printed in short pamphlets and sold in weekly parts. What were these pamphlets known as?

a) Guinea Gruesomes
b) Shilling Shockers
c) Penny Dreadfuls

8 What is the Grand National?

a) an art gallery
b) a horse race
c) a canal

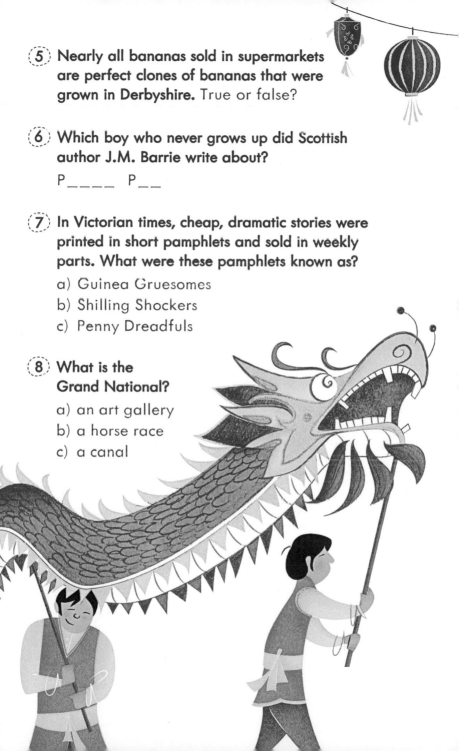

1. Which sport are these men playing? It's thought to have been invented in England, and is a common sight in villages in summer.

    a) baseball   b) cricket   c) rounders

2. I was famous for my suit, bowler hat and cigars. I was known as "The British Bulldog," and I led Britain through the Second World War.

    Who am I?

3. Which town in Wales is known as "the town of books," and hosts a big literary festival each year?

    a) Leigh-on-Sea   b) Hay-on-Wye   c) Overton-on-Dee

4. If you meet the Queen, you should address her as Your...

    a) Highness   b) Ladyship   c) Majesty

5 Who is said to have ridden her horse naked through Coventry to protest against her husband's taxes?

a) Empress Matilda
b) Queen Boudica
c) Lady Godiva

6 ... And who, according to legend, spied on her?

a) Sneaky Pete
b) Peeping Tom
c) Eager Al

7 What is the Royal Mint?

a) the game of polo
b) a herb Elizabeth I liked
c) the maker of British coins

8 What is NOT traditionally served as part of a full English breakfast?

a) boiled egg   b) bacon   c) baked beans

9 Where did Robert the Bruce's Scottish army defeat a much larger English army in 1314?

a) Bannockburn   b) Culloden   c) Naseby

1 What is the scientific instrument above that you can see at Jodrell Bank, southwest of Manchester?

a) space laser   b) TV satellite dish   c) telescope

2 Which of these British authors of fantasy stories was born in Belfast?

a) J.K. Rowling   b) C.S. Lewis   c) J.R.R. Tolkien

3 What is the nickname of the London Underground?

a) the tube   b) the tunnel   c) the pipe

4 If a British person said "it's cats and dogs out there," what would they be talking about?

a) heavy rain   b) angry crowds   c) bad traffic

5 If you wanted to call someone in Great Britain from abroad, which code would you need to dial first?

a) 0022   b) 0044   c) 0066

6 The Houses of Parliament are made up of two "houses." One is the House of Commons, what is the other?

a) House of Uncommons

b) House of Lords

c) House of Cards

7 What is the name of Donald Duck's wealthy Scottish uncle?

a) Scrooge   b) Micawber   c) Fagin

8 I was just an orphan, but I was the only one who could pull the sword from the stone, so I was crowned King of England.

Who am I?

1. In the nursery rhyme, who marched 10,000 men up to the top of the hill and then marched them down again? The Grand Old Duke of...

   a) Kent   b) York   c) Edinburgh

2. The northernmost tip of mainland Ireland is NOT in Northern Ireland.

   True or false?

3. In which seaside town can you find a tower that's based upon the Eiffel Tower in Paris?

   a) Blackpool
   b) Scarborough
   c) Great Yarmouth

4. Where is the London home of the British prime minister?

   a) Buckingham Palace
   b) 10 Downing Street
   c) Houses of Parliament

5. What is "bubble and squeak"?

   a) fried leftover vegetables
   b) a children's cartoon
   c) a hot bath

6 What is the name of the ancient stone landmark that stands in the middle of Salisbury Plain?

a) Shadowstone　　b) Sunhill　c) Stonehenge

7 Which Welsh team has never played in the English Premier League?

a) Cardiff　　　b) Swansea　　　c) Wrexham

8 In 1997, Nelson Mandela met a British pop group and famously said, "They are my heroes." Who was he talking about?

a) One Direction　　b) The Spice Girls　c) Take That

Match each of the British adventurers below to the place on the opposite page that they most famously went to explore.

1) Charles Darwin

2) George Mallory

3) Walter Raleigh

4) James Cook

5) Robert Scott

6) David Livingstone

7) Howard Carter

8) George Vancouver

a) Botany Bay,
   Australia

b) Canada and
   North America

c) Valley of the
   Kings, Egypt

d) Galápagos
   Islands, off
   Ecuador

e) Mount Everest,
   Nepal

f) El Dorado,
   South America

g) South Pole,
   Antarctica

h) Source of the
   Nile, Africa

1 Who, in British politics, famously said, "I don't think there will be a woman prime minister in my lifetime": Winston Churchill **or** Margaret Thatcher?

2 Which sport would you go to watch at Murrayfield?
a) rugby   b) tennis   c) cricket

3 Which English vice admiral defeated the French at Trafalgar, off the coast of Spain, but was fatally shot during the battle?
a) Benbow   b) Hornblower   c) Nelson

4 ... And what was the name of his flagship, now on public display in Portsmouth?
a) *HMS Conquest*
b) *HMS Triumph*
c) *HMS Victory*

5 Which legendary outlaw took from the rich to give to the poor, and lived in Sherwood Forest with his Merry Men?

6 British cows moo in regional accents. True or false?

7 I worked as a ship's surgeon, before writing *A Study in Scarlet*. It didn't earn me much money, but it introduced a very famous character. Who am I? (It's elementary!)

8 The racetrack where the British Formula One Grand Prix is held is called...
a) Goldstone   b) Silverstone   c) Flintstone

9 Which mythical creature is associated with Wales?
a) dragon   b) griffin   c) unicorn

1. **Which capital city is overlooked by the magnificent castle shown above?**
   a) Belfast   b) Edinburgh   c) Cardiff

2. **... And what, in relation to the castle, is Mons Meg:** the hill it's built on **or** a giant siege cannon?

3. **Six ravens are always kept in the Tower of London. What is it said will happen if they ever leave?**
   a) the Thames will change course and destroy London
   b) the ghosts of traitors will rise to have revenge
   c) the kingdom of Great Britain will fall

4. **How many of the British coins below are NOT round?**
   1p   2p   5p   10p   20p   50p   £1   £2

5. **I was born in Belfast, and played for Manchester United. I was known for my fast-paced lifestyle. Pelé called me the greatest player in the world.** Who am I?

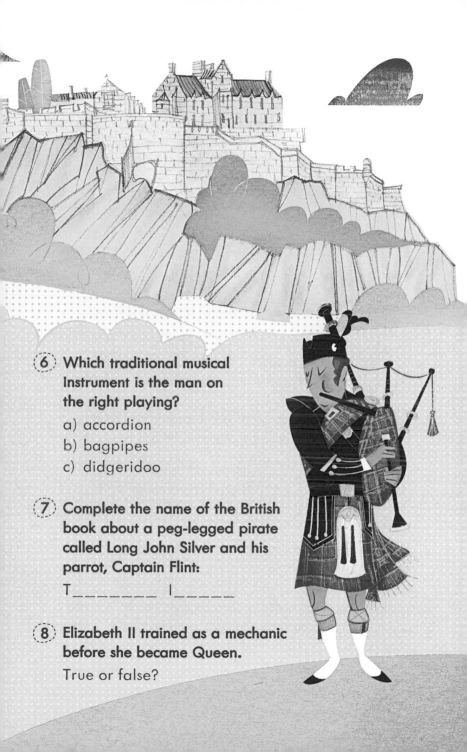

6 Which traditional musical Instrument is the man on the right playing?

   a) accordion

   b) bagpipes

   c) didgeridoo

7 Complete the name of the British book about a peg-legged pirate called Long John Silver and his parrot, Captain Flint:

   T _ _ _ _ _ _ _ _   I _ _ _ _ _

8 Elizabeth II trained as a mechanic before she became Queen.

   True or false?

1 Which engineer designed the steamship the *SS Great Britain* and the Clifton Suspension Bridge in Bristol?
   a) Brunel   b) Stephenson   c) Telford

2 Match these Welsh food words to their English translations:
   a) pysgod a sglodion   1) carrots
   b) ffa pob   2) baked beans
   c) moron   3) fish and chips

3 British soldiers in the First World War were known as Tommies. What name did those soldiers have for Britain?
   a) Blighty   b) Limey   c) Pommy

4 According to legend, what did Canute the Great do to show his courtiers the limits of a king's power?
   a) he ordered a dead man to come back to life
   b) he ordered the Sun to come out at night
   c) he ordered the tide not to come in

5 Cats are the most popular pet in Great Britain. True or false?

6 In Scotland, what's the name of the pouch that's worn over a kilt?
   a) spartan
   b) tartan
   c) sporran

(7) On average, how many cups of tea do the people of Britain drink in a single day?

a) 1.65 million   b) 16.5 million   c) 165 million

(8) Where could you visit the Marble Arch Caves: Central London **or** Northern Ireland?

(9) I have a black and white face, and I'm very good at digging. I live in the countryside across Britain, but you'll only ever see me at night-time. What am I?

(10) Complete these lines from a well-known traditional song: "Are you going to S_ _ _ _ _ _ _ _ _ _ F_ _ _? Parsley, Sage, Rosemary and Thyme."

1 Which port completes the name of these famous chalk cliffs on the English coast? The White Cliffs of...

    a) Bristol   b) Dover   c) Plymouth

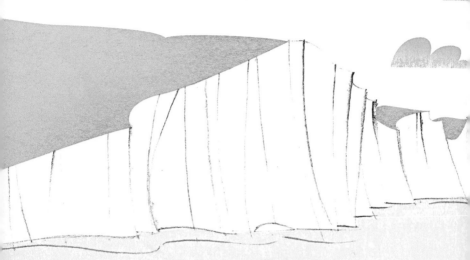

2 ... And, according to a famous old song, what will there be over the cliffs tomorrow?

    a) bluebirds   b) a rainbow   c) storm clouds

3 Can you match each country to its patron saint?

    a) England   1) St. Andrew
    b) Scotland   2) St. David
    c) Wales   3) St. Patrick
    d) Ireland   4) St. George

4 London is the only city in Britain with an underground rail network. True or false?

5 Sir Chris Hoy and Laura Trott have both won numerous Olympic gold medals for Great Britain in which sport?

    a) swimming   b) rowing   c) cycling

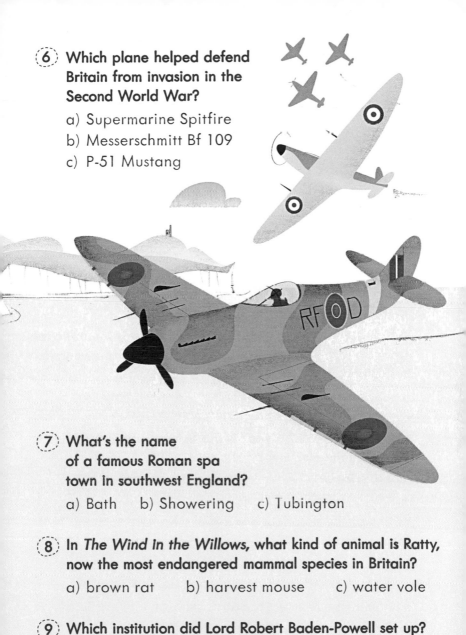

6) Which plane helped defend Britain from invasion in the Second World War?

a) Supermarine Spitfire
b) Messerschmitt Bf 109
c) P-51 Mustang

7) What's the name of a famous Roman spa town in southwest England?

a) Bath   b) Showering   c) Tubington

8) In *The Wind In the Willows*, what kind of animal is Ratty, now the most endangered mammal species in Britain?

a) brown rat   b) harvest mouse   c) water vole

9) Which institution did Lord Robert Baden-Powell set up?

a) Boy Scouts   b) Royal Mail   c) British Airways

10) What were the names of the infamous Edinburgh "body snatchers": Burke and Hare **or** Bonnie and Clyde?

1 Which game are the men above playing? It's the national sport of Wales, although it's said to have been invented in England.

    a) hurling   b) rugby   c) lacrosse

2 On which day of the year is the Scottish song *Auld Lang Syne* traditionally sung?

    a) New Year's Eve   b) Easter Day   c) Halloween

3 Who was the notorious scoundrel who tried to steal the Crown Jewels in 1671: Captain Gore **or** Colonel Blood**?**

4 ... And what did the King do when he was caught?

    a) had him executed for high treason
    b) locked him up with the jewels for life
    c) rewarded him with land worth £500 a year

5 Britain is the largest island in Europe.
    True or false?

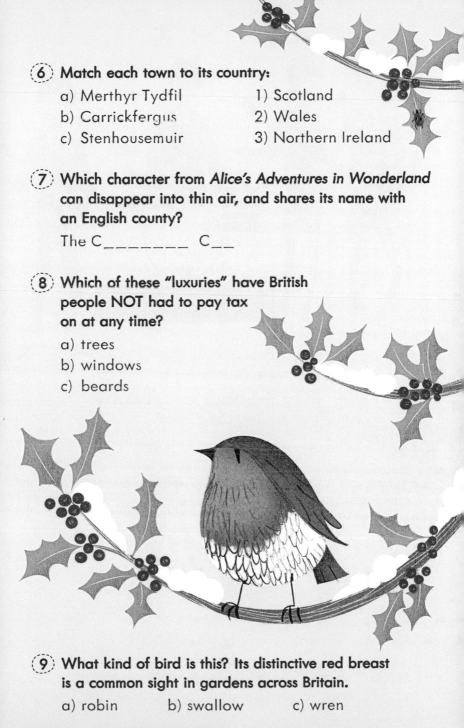

6 Match each town to its country:

a) Merthyr Tydfil   1) Scotland

b) Carrickfergus   2) Wales

c) Stenhousemuir   3) Northern Ireland

7 Which character from *Alice's Adventures in Wonderland* can disappear into thin air, and shares its name with an English county?

The C _ _ _ _ _ _ _ _   C _ _

8 Which of these "luxuries" have British people NOT had to pay tax on at any time?

a) trees

b) windows

c) beards

9 What kind of bird is this? Its distinctive red breast is a common sight in gardens across Britain.

a) robin   b) swallow   c) wren

1. *The Beatles* are the best-selling band of all time.
   Which British city did they come from?
   a) Sheffield   b) Cardiff   c) Liverpool

2. In keeping with a local tradition, what do people in
   Gloucestershire roll down Cooper's Hill each year?
   a) barrels   b) cheese   c) giant dice

3. I was a Native American princess. I married an
   English colonist, but died when I visited England.
   Disney made a film of my story.
   Who am I?

4. Which of England's airports is the busiest in Europe?
   a) Heathrow   b) Gatwick   c) Manchester

5 It is considered bad luck to say the title of Shakespeare's *Macbeth* in a playhouse. What alternative name is it usually given instead?

a) The English Play
b) The Welsh Play
c) The Scottish Play

6 The Menai Strait separates Wales from which island: Alderney **or** Anglesey?

7 What is the popular name of the Houses of Parliament clock tower?

a) Big Ben
b) Little Ben
c) Uncle Ben

8 ... And who, in 1605, was caught trying to blow up the Houses of Parliament?

a) William Wallace
b) Guy Fawkes
c) Wat Tyler

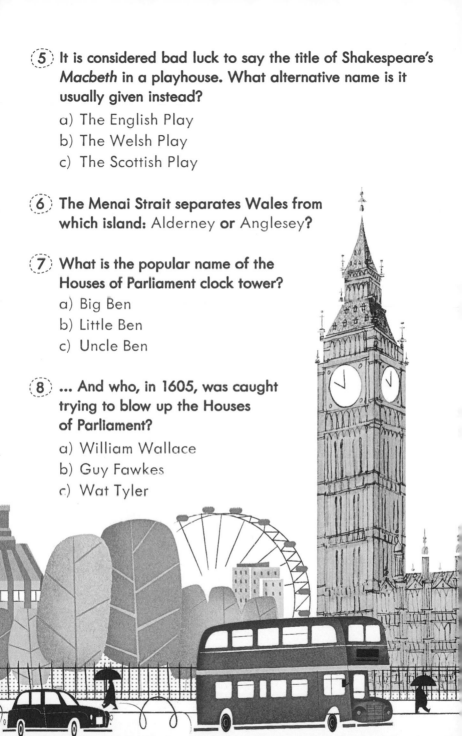

Match each place in England below with the word on the right that completes the name of a current or former Premier League team that comes from there.

1) Crystal

2) Nottingham

3) Aston

4) Manchester

5) Wolverhampton

6) Tottenham

7) Blackburn

8) West Bromwich

9) Charlton

10) Queen's Park

1 Where did the Great Fire of London start when an oven was left burning overnight?

a) Baker Street   b) Chef's Alley   c) Pudding Lane

2 What was the name of the "unbreakable" code that Alan Turing helped to decipher during the Second World War?

a) Sphinx   b) Occult   c) Enigma

3 Which country is home to more people:
Wales **or** Scotland?

4 What kind of boats are the people below pushing along the river using long poles?

a) punts   b) canoes   c) gondolas

5 The Scottish saying "Many a mickle makes a muckle" means the same as which of these English sayings?

  a) save a penny, save a pound
  b) many hands make light work
  c) too many cooks spoil the broth

6 How many birthdays does the Queen have?

  a) one   b) two   c) three

7 Which famous building is this?

  a) St. Albans Abbey
  b) Winchester Cathedral
  c) King's College Chapel

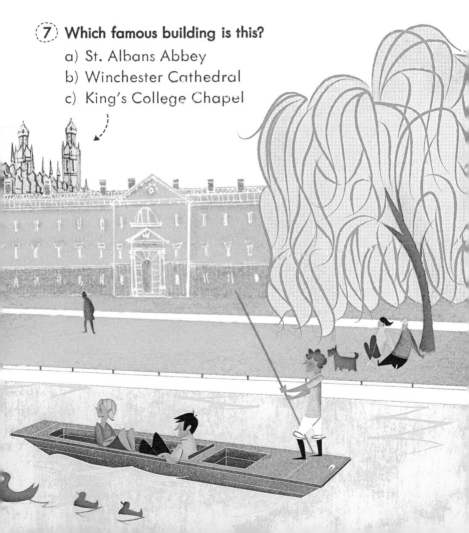

1 Which King of England famously had six wives?
   a) James I
   b) Edward V
   c) Henry VIII

2 My boss is M. My colleague is Q. My codename is 007.
   Who am I?

3 Which ancient language is still spoken in Scotland?
   a) Gaelic
   b) Breton
   c) Manx

4 Who is the head of the Church of England:
   the Pope **or** the Queen?

5 Which anthem do Welsh national teams sing?
   a) Land of Hope and Glory
   b) Land of My Fathers
   c) Land of the Free

6 All prime ministers of Great Britain keep a set of keys to 10 Downing Street for life, after leaving office.
   True or false?

7 The English writer Agatha Christie is the best-selling novelist of all time. What kind of books is she mainly associated with?

a) science fiction   b) adventure   c) crime

8 What is the most common street name in Britain?

a) High Street   b) School Lane   c) Main Road

9 What kind of natural event created the unusual interlocking columns of rock known as the Giant's Causeway?

a) tidal wave
b) earthquake
c) volcanic eruption

1 Which British city has more miles of canal than Venice?

    a) Birmingham   b) Manchester   c) Glasgow

2 Who was the fictional bear found in a London station?

    a) Waterloo   b) Paddington   c) Victoria

3 What is the Scottish slang for a tall, thin person?

    a) Skinny Malinky long-legs

    b) Bony Maloney stilt-legs

    c) Lanky Jimmy spider-shanks

4 Starting with the earliest, can you put these European peoples in order of when they first invaded Britain?

    a) Vikings   b) Romans   c) Normans   d) Saxons

5 Roughly how many people live in Great Britain?

    a) 40 million   b) 60 million   c) 80 million

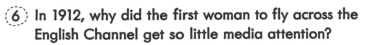

6 In 1912, why did the first woman to fly across the English Channel get so little media attention?

   a) it was frowned upon for women to fly
   b) the *Titanic* had sunk the day before
   c) no one believed that she'd done it

7 Welsh rarebit is the name of one of Wales's best-known traditional dishes. What is it?

   a) lamb steak   b) rabbit stew   c) cheese on toast

8 According to legend, which heroic figure killed a dragon: St. George **or** Sir Lancelot?

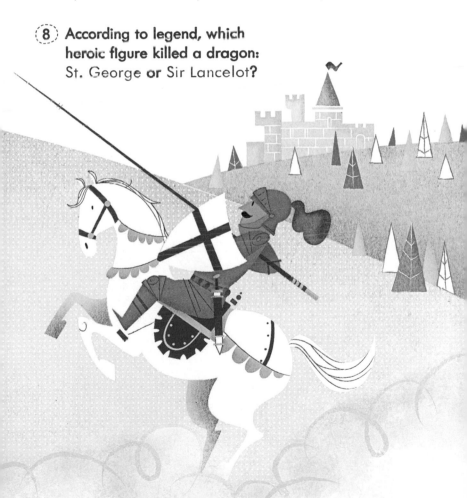

1 Match these Northern Irish slang words to their meanings:

a) craic 1) broken
b) eejit 2) walk
c) dander 3) fun
d) banjaxed 4) idiot

2 Which animal can you NOT find in British woods?

a) red squirrel   b) wild boar   c) common wolf

3 What was the nurse Florence Nightingale known as?

a) The Lady with the Lamp
b) The Angel of Crimea
c) The Soldiers' Saint

4 Which London train station is the busiest in Britain?

a) Euston
b) Waterloo
c) King's Cross

5 In which stadium is the FA Cup final played?

a) Wembley
b) Old Trafford
c) Villa Park

6 The Union Jack is perfectly symmetrical.
True or false?

7 According to legend, what did Alfred the Great burn?

a) his finger   b) some cakes   c) the Viking fleet

8 What was the name of the brigade that suffered heavy casualties in an infamous cavalry charge at the Battle of Balaclava, during the Crimean War?

a) The Heavy Brigade
b) The Light Brigade
c) The Fire Brigade

9 Who led a fierce revolt against English rule in Wales, and was the last native Welshman to hold the title Prince of Wales: Owain Glyndŵr **or** Geoffrey of Monmouth?

10 What was Englishman Roger Bannister the first to do?

a) climb Mount Everest without oxygen
b) swim across the English Channel
c) run a mile in under four minutes

11 J.K. Rowling wrote much of the early *Harry Potter* books while sitting in The Elephant House café in which British capital city?

a) Edinburgh   b) Belfast   c) Cardiff

1 What is Aviemore in Scotland particularly known for?

a) skiing   b) surfing   c) bungee jumping

2 The motto of the English monarch is in which language?

a) English   b) French   c) Latin

3 I led the English Civil War against Charles I, and became Lord Protector of the country. After I died, Charles II had my head put on a stake.

Who am I?

4 Which of these is NOT a real place in the British Isles?

a) Cardigan   b) Jersey   c) Sweater

5 In a book by Bram Stoker, which monster terrorized the northern town of Whitby: Frankenstein **or** Dracula?

6 Nicholas Breakspear is the only Englishman ever to have held which position?

   a) US President   b) Pope   c) Prince of Wales

7 Where would you be most likely to hear someone say "She's a bonnie wee lass, that bairn of yours"?

   a) Ipswich   b) Motherwell   c) Swansea

8 In 2015, which British driver won his third Formula One World Championship: Lewis Hamilton **or** Jenson Button?

9 What's the name of the highest mountain in Great Britain?

   a) Bob Nevis
   b) Bill Nevis
   c) Ben Nevis

1 If a Welshman said "bore da" to you, what would he be saying?

   a) I'm bored   b) good morning   c) my pig is dead

2 In Britain, no one lives more than 70 miles from the sea. True or false?

3 The village of Badminton, in Gloucestershire, is a famous venue for which sport?

   a) badminton   b) cricket   c) horse riding

4 Which Northern Irish actor has appeared in both a *Star Wars* film and a *Batman* film?

   a) James Nesbitt   b) Liam Neeson   c) Sam Neill

5 What was the deadly plague that killed around a third of the English population in the 1300s?

   a) Black Death   b) Red Death   c) White Death

6 I'm a wooden puppet with a cruel, nasal voice. A hungry crocodile tries to steal my sausages. My wife's name is Judy. Who am I?

7 On a road map of Great Britain, motorways are usually...

    a) blue   b) red   c) green

8 Henry III kept an exotic pet, given to him by the King of Norway, in the Tower of London. What was it?

    a) a tiger   b) a giraffe   c) a polar bear

9 Who wrote the poem *Daffodils* after he came upon a patch of them while walking in the Lake District: William Wordsworth **or** Christopher Commacost?

10 From a beach in Cornwall in southern England, which country are you facing if you look directly west?

    a) Ireland
    b) Canada
    c) United States

1 What is the English folk dance in which the dancers attach bells to their legs and twirl handkerchiefs?

    a) Foxtrot   b) Morris dance   c) Can-can

2 Can you match each surname to the country that it is mainly associated with?

    a) Macdonald   1) Wales

    b) Griffiths   2) England

    c) Smith   3) Scotland

3 Which Welsh singer is said to have the voice of an angel: Charlotte Church **or** Shirley Bassey?

4 "We are not amused" is a phrase associated with which queen?

    a) Anne   b) Elizabeth I   c) Victoria

(5) What is the name of the traditional festival where English villagers dance around a pole on the village green?

a) Eisteddfod   b) Hogmanay   c) May Day

(6) What was unusual about William the Conqueror's funeral?

a) his body exploded
b) the bishop died during it
c) he woke up because he wasn't dead

(7) Which city in Great Britain is the furthest north?

a) Glasgow   b) Newcastle   c) Inverness

(8) Complete the name of the infamous highwayman who is said to have ridden a horse called Black Bess:

D _ _ _   T _ _ _ _ _

(9) Who was the Scottish freedom fighter, nicknamed Braveheart, that defeated the English at the Battle of Stirling Bridge: Robert the Bruce **or** William Wallace**?**

(10) The Channel Tunnel was begun in the 1880s. True or false?

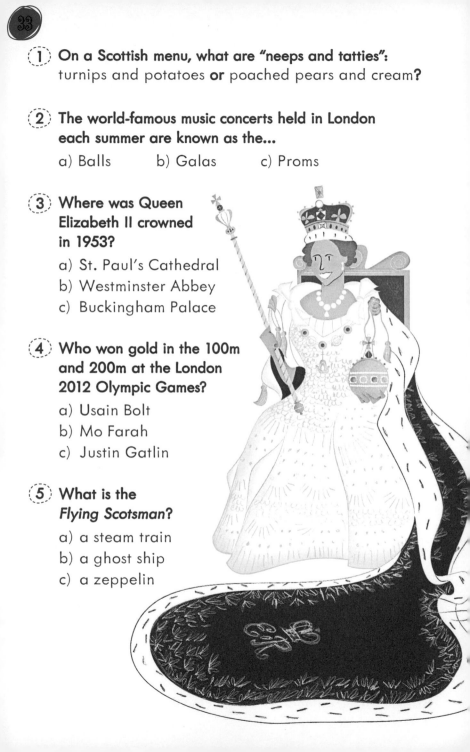

1 On a Scottish menu, what are "neeps and tatties": turnips and potatoes **or** poached pears and cream**?**

2 The world-famous music concerts held in London each summer are known as the...
a) Balls   b) Galas   c) Proms

3 Where was Queen Elizabeth II crowned in 1953?
a) St. Paul's Cathedral
b) Westminster Abbey
c) Buckingham Palace

4 Who won gold in the 100m and 200m at the London 2012 Olympic Games?
a) Usain Bolt
b) Mo Farah
c) Justin Gatlin

5 What is the *Flying Scotsman*?
a) a steam train
b) a ghost ship
c) a zeppelin

6 Where is Llanfairpwllgwyngyllgogerychwyrndrobwll-llantysiliogogogoch, the village with the longest place name in Europe?

a) Northern Ireland
b) Scotland
c) Wales

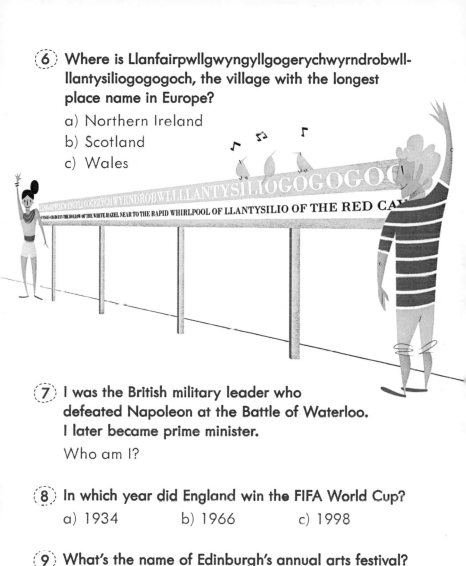

7 I was the British military leader who defeated Napoleon at the Battle of Waterloo. I later became prime minister.

Who am I?

8 In which year did England win the FIFA World Cup?

a) 1934   b) 1966   c) 1998

9 What's the name of Edinburgh's annual arts festival?

a) the Braid   b) the Fringe   c) the Plait

10 Why were some of the women who were part of the war effort during the First World War known as "canaries"?

a) they sang all day as they worked
b) they were sent to work down in the mines
c) their skin turned yellow from working with chemicals

Match each of the British sayings below to the correct meaning on the opposite page.

2) An arm and a leg

3) Bob's your uncle

1) Chalk and cheese

4) Nineteen to the dozen

5) Chuffed to bits

7) Not cricket

6) Pigs can fly

9) The bee's knees

8) Not my cup of tea

10) Parky

1 Which travel company began life in the 1840s by taking the people of Britain on day-trips to the sea?

a) Thomas Cook   b) British Rail   c) The AA

2 In the days of the British Empire, the areas under British rule were shown on world maps in...

a) green   b) pink   c) red, white and blue

3 What are the names of the popular TV duo who present *Britain's Got Talent*: Ant and Dec **or** Dick and Dom?

4 If you visited the British Museum, which of these things from ancient history would you NOT see?

a) The Rosetta Stone
b) Cleopatra's Needle
c) The Elgin Marbles

5 Which take-away meal, traditionally wrapped in newspaper, is one of the most popular in Britain?

a) fish and chips   b) pizza   c) chicken nuggets

6 In the *Harry Potter* books, from which London station do young witches and wizards catch the Hogwarts Express?

    a) King's Cross   b) Paddington   c) Waterloo

7 What is Great Britain's most common butterfly called?

    a) Radish Red   b) Pea Green   c) Cabbage White

8 In the Second World War, Brighton Pier was shut in case Germany used it to land troops and invade. True or false?

1 What are the 20 or so most important politicians in the British government collectively known as?

a) the Bureau   b) the Cabinet   c) the Chair

2 According to legend, what did the Irish giant Finn MacCool disguise himself as in order to scare off a Scottish giant who had come to fight him?

a) a dragon   b) a tree   c) a baby

3 Which member of the Spice Girls did David Beckham marry in 1999?

a) Sporty Spice   b) Baby Spice   c) Posh Spice

4 The giant hill figure below was carved into a hillside in Uffington roughly 3,000 years ago. What kind of animal is it generally thought to be?

a) a horse   b) a lion   c) a wolf

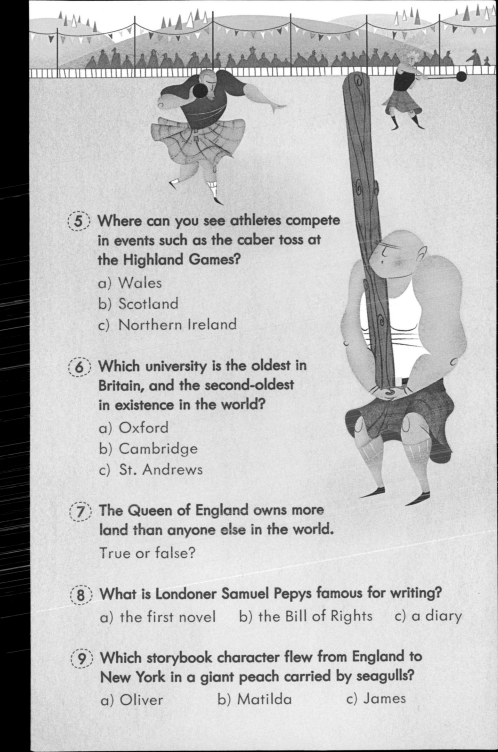

5 Where can you see athletes compete in events such as the caber toss at the Highland Games?

a) Wales
b) Scotland
c) Northern Ireland

6 Which university is the oldest in Britain, and the second-oldest in existence in the world?

a) Oxford
b) Cambridge
c) St. Andrews

7 The Queen of England owns more land than anyone else in the world.
True or false?

8 What is Londoner Samuel Pepys famous for writing?

a) the first novel   b) the Bill of Rights   c) a diary

9 Which storybook character flew from England to New York in a giant peach carried by seagulls?

a) Oliver   b) Matilda   c) James

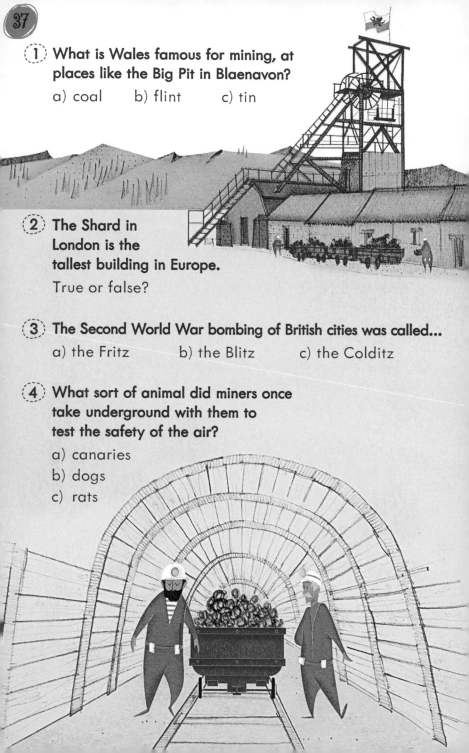

1) What is Wales famous for mining, at places like the Big Pit in Blaenavon?

a) coal   b) flint   c) tin

2) The Shard in London is the tallest building in Europe.

True or false?

3) The Second World War bombing of British cities was called...

a) the Fritz   b) the Blitz   c) the Colditz

4) What sort of animal did miners once take underground with them to test the safety of the air?

a) canaries
b) dogs
c) rats

(5) **What is the name of the estuary on the east coast of England where King John's treasure is said to be lost?**
   a) the Bath   b) the Rinse   c) the Wash

(6) **In 1649, King Charles I was tried and executed for high treason, but which of the statements below is NOT true?**
   a) Charles wore two shirts so he wouldn't shiver
   b) his judge wore a metal-lined hat in case he was shot
   c) the crowd wore hoods to avoid touching royal blood

(7) **Which animal, shown below, was voted Great Britain's best-loved wild species in a 2013 poll?**

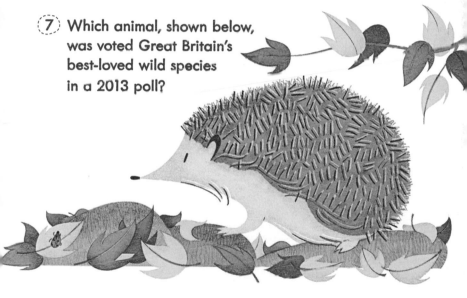

(8) **Complete these lines from a famous traditional song:**
   "But me and my true love will never meet again,
   On the bonnie, bonnie banks of..."
   a) Loch Lomond   b) Moon River   c) Wast Water

(9) **Which British TV show is about an alien who travels through time in a blue phone box called the TARDIS?**
   a) Doctor When   b) Doctor Who   c) Doctor Why

Answers

1 **1.** b **2.** Sir Isaac Newton **3.** a **4.** c **5.** The Magna Carta (It was a document that limited the king's power. The Domesday Book was a great survey carried out by William the Conqueror in 1086 to see what property people had and how much it was worth.) **6.** a **7.** b **8.** c

2 **1.** c (They are called "bangers" because when the First World War caused meat shortages, they had a high water content and were likely to burst when cooked.) **2.** The London Eye **3.** True (They are not used, but are kept in the Bank of England to back up the value of the currency. There are also banknotes for £100 million.) **4.** c (in the book *Gulliver's Travels* by Jonathan Swift) **5.** a **6.** b **7.** Celtic and Rangers **8.** c (The name comes from "suffrage," which means the right to vote.) **9.** a **10.** c

3 **1.** Roald Dahl **2.** the Bank of England **3.** a **4.** c **5.** b (The record was broken in 2016 when Paul Pogba signed for Manchester United for £89 million.) **6.** the Jolly Roger (His real name was John Rackham. He was a pirate captain, famous for having two female crew members – Anne Bonny and Mary Read. Some sources also credit him with contributing to the design of the Jolly Roger that we all know today.) **7.** b

4 **1.** c **2.** a **3.** b **4.** b **5.** b **6.** c **7.** nine days **8.** William Shakespeare **9.** c (Only 12 astronauts have walked on the Moon, all of them American.) **10.** Great Snoring (It's in Norfolk.)

5 **1.** False (The Emerald Isle is a nickname for Ireland.) **2.** b (It's nothing like bread, and is sometimes known as Welsh caviar.) **3.** b **4.** a **5.** c **6.** January 25th (to celebrate the birthday of Scotland's most famous poet, Robert Burns) **7.** b (It's based on *A Christmas Carol*.) **8.** a **9.** c **10.** c

6 1. a (accompanied by James Bond) 2. a 3. b 4. Diana, Princess of Wales 5. c (It is the highest military decoration in Britain, and is awarded for extreme acts of bravery in the face of the enemy.) 6. Blue Peter (It first aired in 1958.) 7. a 8. c ("Unready" is actually a mistranslation of an Old English word that meant "badly advised.") 9. b

7 1. c (or His Majesty's Ship when there is a king) 2. b 3. b 4. False (Although widely believed to be true, there is no law against this. It is treason to commit an act with the intention of deposing the monarch, but putting a stamp on upside down would not be enough to qualify.) 5. b 6. a (Ships used to race to try to win a bonus for delivering the first tea shipment of the year. *Ariel* was first back, but the tide meant *Taeping* was able to enter her dock first. *Taeping* claimed the victory, but the two ships split the bonus between them. The Great Tea Race of 1866, as it is known, was the last year such a race took place as steamships began to take over.) 7. c 8. b 9. a (They are made from real bearskins.) 10. c

8 1. c 2. a 3. c 4. a (Oriel and Somerville are both real Oxford colleges.) 5. The Lake District 6. b 7. b (The trophy was stolen while on display, four months before England hosted the tournament, but was recovered seven days later.) 8. c (Cranachan is a dessert made with whipped cream, raspberries, honey, whisky and oatmeal.)

9 1. c 2. Sherlock Holmes 3. Rory McIlroy 4. b 5. a 6. c 7. a 8. b

10 1. b (They took the titles of the Duke and Duchess of Cambridge.) 2. a 3. b (Englishman Christopher Merret documented the process to make sparkling wine almost 40 years before it was claimed that Dom Pérignon had invented it.) 4. b 5. Banksy (His identity is unknown, possibly because graffiti is often illegal. However, his works are highly valued. Pudsey is the mascot for Children In Need.) 6. c 7. b 8. c 9. tiger (spelled "tyger" in the poem)

11 **1.** a **2.** Fantastic Mr. Fox (in the book of the same name by Roald Dahl) **3.** b **4.** c (Its full name is The Royal and Ancient Golf Club of St. Andrews.) **5.** jousting **6.** the left (the same as everywhere else in the British Isles) **7.** c (He was nicknamed "Capability" because he told his clients that their property had the capability to improve.) **8.** a (It was originally made from wood, and then rebuilt using stone in the 1100s.)

12 1d, 2f, 3a, 4c, 5b, 6e

13 1b, 2e, 3f, 4a, 5c, 6d

14 **1.** b **2.** a2, b3, c1 **3.** bowls (He is said to have been playing a game on Plymouth Hoe, and to have remarked that there was plenty of time to finish the game and still beat the Spaniards. However, there is no known witness to him actually saying this.) **4.** a (It takes place during the Chinese New Year celebrations.) **5.** True (Some imported bananas were grown at Chatsworth House in Derbyshire. When a disease devastated Gros Michel bananas in the 1950s, these Cavendish bananas, named after the 6th Duke of Devonshire, became the most popular.) **6.** Peter Pan **7.** c (They were so named because they cost just a penny and often contained dark, gruesome tales.) **8.** b (It takes place every year at Aintree, in Liverpool, and has the highest prize fund of any jump race in Europe.)

15 **1.** b **2.** Sir Winston Churchill **3.** b **4.** c (and after that, Ma'am) **5.** c **6.** b **7.** c **8.** a (The eggs in a full English breakfast are either fried or scrambled.) **9.** a

16 **1.** c (It "sees" by detecting radio waves emitted by objects in space, which is why it looks like a huge satellite dish.) **2.** b **3.** a **4.** a **5.** b **6.** b **7.** a **8.** King Arthur

17 **1.** b **2.** True (It's Malin Head in the Republic of Ireland.) **3.** a (It was built in 1894, five years after the Eiffel Tower, and is 158m (518ft) tall.) **4.** b **5.** a (The main ingredients are usually potato and cabbage, and it gets its name from the noises it makes as it's cooked.) **6.** c **7.** c **8.** b

18 1d, 2e, 3f, 4a, 5g, 6h, 7c, 8b

19 **1.** Margaret Thatcher (who went on to become Britain's first female prime minister) **2.** a **3.** c **4.** c **5.** Robin Hood **6.** True (Language specialists have suggested that cows moo slightly differently in local areas, possibly picking up on the accents of the farmers who rear them.) **7.** Sir Arthur Conun Doyle (*A Study in Scarlet* was the first story featuring Sherlock Holmes.) **8.** b **9.** a

20 **1.** b **2.** a giant siege cannon **3.** c **4.** two (The 20p and the 50p coins both have seven sides.) **5.** George Best **6.** b **7.** *Treasure Island* **8.** True (In 1945, towards the end of the Second World War, she joined the Women's Auxiliary Territorial Service and trained as a driver and a mechanic.)

21 **1.** a **2.** a3, b2, c1 **3.** a **4.** c **5.** False (Cats are the most popular pet worldwide, but in Britain more people have dogs.) **6.** c **7.** c **8.** Northern Ireland (They are named after a nearby natural arch of limestone, and have nothing to do with Marble Arch in London.) **9.** a badger **10.** Scarborough Fair

22 **1.** b **2.** a **3.** a4, b1, c2, d3 **4.** False (Glasgow also has one.) **5.** c **6.** a **7.** a **8.** c **9.** a (He formed them in 1908, and he and his sister, Agnes, also formed the Girl Guides in 1909.) **10.** Burke and Hare (In 1828, they murdered 16 people in Edinburgh over a period of about ten months, selling the bodies to a doctor who used them for dissection and anatomy lectures. Bonnie and Clyde were American outlaws.)

23 **1.** b (It was supposedly invented at Rugby School in 1823 when William Webb Ellis picked up the ball and ran with it during a game of soccer.) **2.** a (It is traditionally sung at midnight to see in the new year.) **3.** Colonel Blood **4.** c (Some say the King feared an uprising from Blood's followers, while others think he had a fondness for scoundrels.) **5.** True **6.** a2, b3, c1 **7.** The Cheshire Cat **8.** a (Taxes on beards existed in Henry VIII's and Elizabeth I's reigns, and a tax on windows was in place from the late 1600s until 1851.) **9.** a

24 1. c 2. b (Double Gloucester cheese is used.) 3. Pocahontas 4. a 5. c 6. Anglesey 7. a (The tower is actually called the Elizabeth Tower. Big Ben is the name of the bell inside, but is commonly used for the whole tower.) 8. b

25 1j, 2h, 3e, 4d, 5c, 6b, 7g, 8i, 9a, 10f

26 1. c 2. c 3. Scotland (Its population is roughly 5.3 million; Wales's is roughly 3.1 million.) 4. a 5. a (A "mickle" is a small amount, and a "muckle" is a large amount, so it means you can accumulate a great deal with lots of small savings.) 6. b (George II started the tradition in 1748. His actual birthday was in November, so he created an official birthday in Spring, when the weather would be nicer for his birthday parade.) 7. c (It's part of Cambridge University, and is famous for its televised carol service at Christmas each year.)

27 1. c 2. James Bond 3. a 4. the Queen (The monarch has been head of the Church of England ever since Henry VIII split from the Roman Catholic Church so that he could divorce his first wife, Catherine of Aragon.) 5. b 6. False (In fact, prime ministers don't have keys at all because the door to 10 Downing Street cannot be opened from the outside; there is always someone on the inside to unlock it.) 7. c (She created Hercule Poirot and Miss Marple.) 8. a 9. c

28 1. a 2. b (He was named after the station.) 3. a 4. b, d, a, c 5. b 6. b (American pilot Harriet Quimby made the flight from Dover to Calais in 59 minutes.) 7. c 8. St. George

29 1. a3, b4, c2, d1 2. c (Wild wolves no longer live in Britain.) 3. a 4. b 5. a 6. False 7. b (The legend says a peasant woman gave Alfred shelter when he was fleeing the invading Danes. She asked him to watch some cakes she was cooking, but he was too preoccupied thinking about his kingdom and let them burn.) 8. b (commemorated in the poem *The Charge of the Light Brigade* by Alfred Lord Tennyson) 9. Owain Glyndŵr 10. c (In 1954, he ran a time of 3 minutes 59.4 seconds.) 11. a

30 **1.** a **2.** b (It's "Dieu et mon droit," which means "God and my right." After the Norman invasion in 1066, French was the main language of the royal court for several centuries.) **3.** Oliver Cromwell **4.** c (Cardigan is in Wales, and Jersey is one of the Channel Islands.) **5.** Dracula **6.** b **7.** b (in Scotland) **8.** Lewis Hamilton **9.** c

31 **1.** b **2.** True (The Ordnance Survey has calculated that the furthest point from the sea in Britain is a farm near Coton in the Elms in Derbyshire, 70 miles from the sea.) **3.** c **4.** b **5.** a **6.** Mr. Punch **7.** a **8.** c **9.** William Wordsworth **10.** b

32 **1.** b **2.** a3, b1, c2 **3.** Charlotte Church **4.** c (She supposedly said it at a dinner party when a guest made a rude joke.) **5.** c (It's a celebration of Spring, held on May 1st.) **6.** a **7.** c **8.** Dick Turpin **9.** William Wallace **10.** True (Work was stopped, though, because it was feared that the French might use it to invade England. Today's tunnel was opened in 1994.)

33 **1.** turnips and potatoes **2.** c **3.** b (English and British monarchs have been crowned there since 1066.) **4.** a **5.** a **6.** c (Its name means St. Mary's Church in the hollow of the white hazel near to the rapid whirlpool of Llantysilio of the red cave.) **7.** The Duke of Wellington **8.** b **9.** b **10.** c (They made the artillery shells, and the long exposure to nitric acid in the TNT turned their skin yellow.)

34 1j, 2g, 3d, 4a, 5i, 6b, 7e, 8h, 9c, 10f

35 **1.** a **2.** b **3.** Ant and Dec **4.** b (Cleopatra's Needle is an Ancient Egyptian obelisk that stands on the bank of the Thames.) **5.** a (Greaseproof paper is now used so that newspaper ink doesn't get into the food, but many places still add a layer of newspaper too.) **6.** a (from platform nine and three-quarters) **7.** c **8.** True

1. b **2.** c (The Scottish giant thought how much bigger the baby's father must be, and fled back to Scotland!) **3.** c (They are often called "Posh and Becks.") **4.** a **5.** b **6.** a (The University of Bologna is the only surviving university that's older.) **7.** True (Large parts of Canada and Australia (the second and sixth largest countries in the world) are still "Crown Land" from the days of the British Empire. The land is owned by the Crown, which is headed by the Queen, although she does not own it personally.) **8.** c (His diary famously documents the Great Fire of London.) **9.** c (in *James and the Giant Peach* by Roald Dahl)

 1. a **2.** False (It is the tallest building in Western Europe, but there are three buildings in Moscow that are taller.) **3.** b **4.** a (Toxic gases affected the birds before the miners, indicating it was unsafe.) **5.** c (In 1216, John sent his baggage train, including his Crown Jewels, along a route that included a causeway that was only usable at low tide. When the tide came in too fast, the jewels were lost to the sea.) **6.** c (In fact, many of those watching dipped handkerchiefs into the King's blood because it was thought it would bring good luck.) **7.** the hedgehog **8.** a **9.** b

With thanks to Simon Tudhope

Edited by Kirsteen Robson and Sam Taplin

First published in 2017 by Usborne Publishing Ltd, 83–85 Saffron Hill, London ECIN 8RT, England.